Ruff
and the
Mother
Bird

Vesta J. Seek

Illustrated by
Deborah G. Wilson

Chariot Books™
David C. Cook Publishing Co.

To the memory of my mother,
who is the "Janie" in the stories.

Thank you, Christine, for all your typing.
V.S.

For Neisha and her dog, Jake

D.W.

Chariot Books™ is an imprint of David C. Cook Publishing Co.
David C. Cook Publishing Co., Elgin, Illinois 60120
David C. Cook Publishing Co., Weston, Ontario

OLD RUFF AND THE MOTHER BIRD
©1991 by Vesta Seek for text and Deborah G. Wilson for illustrations

Designed by Donna Kae Nelson
First Printing, 1991
Printed in Singapore
95 94 93 92 91   5 4 3 2 1

Library of Congress Cataloging-in-Publication Data
Seek, Vesta
        Old Ruff and the mother bird/ Vesta Seek; illustrated by Deborah
G. Wilson.
                p.   cm. — (On my own books)
        Summary: Janie prays for the opportunity to see the offspring of
an unusual bird whose babies often move to a new location after
hatching from their eggs.
            ISBN 1-55513-361-4
            [1. Killdeer--Fiction. 2. Birds--Fiction. 3. Christian Life--
Fiction.]   I. Wilson, Deborah G., ill. II Title.
PZ7.S451601   1990
[E]--dc20   89-25264
                                                                CIP
                                                                AC

"Come on, Old Ruff,"
said Janie one day.
"Let's go for a run."
They ran from the farm house
to the woods and back again.

Now Janie wanted to rest.

But Old Ruff still wanted to play.

He jumped up and down.

"Come on, Janie," he seemed to say.

"I want you to play with me."

"All right," laughed Janie.

"See this stick?"

Janie threw the stick

over by the woods.

"Get it, Ruff," she said.

Ruff ran after the stick.

He picked it up

and ran back to Janie.

Next Janie threw the stick

over by the barn.

When Old Ruff went to get it,

he saw a bird in the grass.

The bird was hopping

this way and that way,

one wing up and

one wing down.

Janie saw the bird, too.

"Oh, my," she said.

"I think that bird is hurt!

Here, Ruff.

Come away from the bird.

You stay here.

I'll go and see if I can help it."

Janie walked through the grass.

The bird was still hopping

this way and that way,

one wing up and one wing down.

It seemed to call,

"Help me! Help me! Help me!"

"Here little bird," said Janie.

But the bird went hopping on,

and she could not get near it.

Then the bird flew away.

"That's funny," said Janie.

"I thought it was hurt.

I thought it could not fly."

Janie went back near the porch

and lay down on the grass.

She lay still for a long time.

She looked up at the sky.

The clouds were so white.

The sky was so blue.

But Old Ruff did not want

to look at clouds.

He wanted to play.

He got the stick again

and took it to Janie.

"All right," laughed Janie.

"I will play with you."

She threw the stick over by the barn.

Old Ruff ran to get it.

And there was that bird again!

Hopping this way and that way,

one wing up and one wing down!

Old Ruff ran after the bird.

"No! Ruff, no!" said Janie.

"Come here and sit.

I'll see if I can help."

Ruff came and sat still.

Janie walked slowly

through the grass.

The bird seemed to be calling,

"Help me! Help me! Help me!"

But it went hopping on and on,

and Janie could not get near it.

"Don't go away, little bird," called Janie.

"I want to help you."

But the bird flew away again.

"Well, well!

What do you think about that?"

Janie said to Old Ruff.

"Is it hurt, or isn't it?"

Soon Pa and the brothers

came in from work.

Janie told them all about

the funny bird.

"Oh," said Pa, "I think

that is a mother killdeer.

She must have some eggs there.

She wants you to think she is hurt.

If you go after her, she will lead

you away from her eggs.

"Oh, I see," said Janie.

"Do you think we can find the eggs?"

"We can look," said Pa.

"They will be down in the grass."

After dinner Janie and Pa

and the brothers

walked to the barn.

And there was the bird in the grass,

hopping this way and that way!

One wing up and one wing down!

She seemed to be calling,

"Help me! Help me! Help me!"

"Oh, no, little bird," laughed Janie.

"You cannot fool us this time.

We know you are not hurt.

But where are your eggs?"

Pa said, "They must be here,

but I can't see them."

He looked and looked.

The brothers looked and looked, too.

"Well," said Pa, "I guess we can't find them.

Come on, boys, we have work to do."

Pa and the boys went back to the fields.

Janie went back and lay down

on the porch.

She put her head in Ma's lap.

Soon she went to sleep.

Ma rested her head

and went to sleep, too.

When Janie woke up, she said,

"I want to go

and look for the eggs again."

Ma watched her go.

Then Ma saw the killdeer

jump up from a spot by the road.

It was hopping away,

going this way and that way,

one wing up and one wing down.

Ma did not look at the killdeer.

She just looked at the spot by the road

where she first saw the killdeer.

Then she walked up the road

looking all the time at that spot.

When she got to the spot,

she looked down.

"Come over here, Janie," she called.

And there on the road by the grass

they saw four little eggs.

Four little eggs that looked like

little round stones.

"Oh, Ma," Janie said softly.

"I want to hold one of the eggs."

"If you do that," said Ma,

"the mother bird may not come back.

We want her to sit on the eggs

and keep them warm."

"All right," said Janie.

"I will not hold them, but I want

to come back and see them."

"Look around so you can find

this spot again," said Ma.

That night when Janie saw Pa coming

from the field, she ran to him.

"Pa, we did find the eggs," she said.

"I will go every day and look at them.

Someday I will see the baby birds."

"No," said Pa. "I do not think

you will ever see a baby killdeer."

"Why not?" asked Janie.

"When the baby killdeer

come out of the eggs,

they can run," Pa said.

"They will run away in the grass,

and you will never see them.

That's part of God's plan, Janie.

He wants them to be safe."

This made Janie feel a little sad

and a little happy at the same time.

Pa knew so much.

He knew about things like this.

But she wanted so much

to see the baby birds.

Every day Janie thought about it.

She talked it over with Old Ruff.

"Do you think the baby birds

will look like the mother killdeer?"

she asked.

Every day Janie went to look at the eggs.

Every day Mother Killdeer saw Janie come.

Mother Killdeer got to know Janie.

She seemed to think,

"Janie will not take my eggs."

One day Janie saw some little cracks

in two of the eggs.

"The little birds will come out soon,"

she told Old Ruff.

"I will go and look in the morning.

Maybe I will get to see the baby birds."

That night Janie did not sleep much.

She wanted morning to come.

She lay in her bed

and talked softly to God.

"Please, God," she said, "I do want

to see the baby birds.

You know I will not hurt them.

Mother Killdeer knows that, too.

Please, God!"

In the morning Janie got out of bed.

Ma and Pa were not up.

But it was getting light outside.

Old Ruff was on the porch.

"Stay, Ruff," said Janie.

He did not move.

Janie walked slowly up the road by the barn.

Mother Killdeer was there.

She sat and looked at Janie.

Janie sat down and looked at

Mother Killdeer.

Then the mother bird got up and hopped about

a little, but she did not go away.

Janie sat very still.

Then in a flash, four fluffy little birds

jumped up and looked at her.

Janie was too happy to talk.

But she thought, *Oh, you dear little things.*

You look so much like your mother.

And it seemed as if the little birds

were thinking, too.

They looked at Janie, then at each other

as if to say, "What big animal is this?"

Let's get away from here, fast!"

And then they were gone in the grass,

just as Pa had said they would.

Janie looked and looked,

but she could not find them.

Dear little birds, you are gone,

thought Janie.

But I did get to see you!

As Janie slowly walked back to the house,

God seemed to be there with her.

"Thank You," she said softly.

"I will never forget this day!"